This book belongs to

. . . .

For my great friend Lorna and her beautiful daughters. C.W.

For my delightfully noisy nibblers, Lori and Jamie. R.B.

This paperback edition first published in 2014 by Andersen Press Ltd.
First published in Great Britain in 2013 by Andersen Press Ltd.,
20 Vauxhall Bridge Road, London SW1V 2SA.
Published in Australia by Random House Australia Pty.,
Level 3, 100 Pacific Highway, North Sydney, NSW 2060.

10   9   8   7   6   5   4   3   2   1

British Library Cataloguing in Publication Data available.

ISBN 978 1 84939 649 3

FSC
www.fsc.org

MIX
Paper from
responsible sources
FSC® C012700

What Noise Does a Rabbit Make?

Written by **Carrie Weston**

Illustrated by **Richard Byrne**

ANDERSEN PRESS

In the still of the night,
   just before dawn,
      slowly and silently . . .

. . . the meadow filled
with rabbits.

Raggety-Taggle
and his brothers
and his sisters,
his aunts,
and his uncles,
all nibbled peacefully.

But as the sun came up . . .

Cock-a-doodle-do!

trumpeted the **cockerel.**

Moo!

went the **cows.**

Neigh!

said the horses.

Baa-baaaaaaaaa!

the sheep joined in.

Oink! Oink!

grunted the pigs.

Meow!

went the cat in search
of her breakfast.

Woof!
Woof!

barked the dog as the farmer
started his tractor.

Chu-chu-brrr-chug,
chug, chug!

The farm rang out with noises.

Raggety-Taggle listened with his long ears and thought very hard.

Tweet ~~Tweet~~

"Just what noise **does** a rabbit make?"

he wondered.

Raggety-Taggle tapped
his foot and thought.

Thump - thump -
thumpety-thump.

A long way off,
in the tall grass,
two ears pricked up.
A tail flicked.

Two eyes blinked.

Whiskers twitched.
The cat licked her lips.

Thump - thump - thumpety - thump!

went Raggety-Taggle.

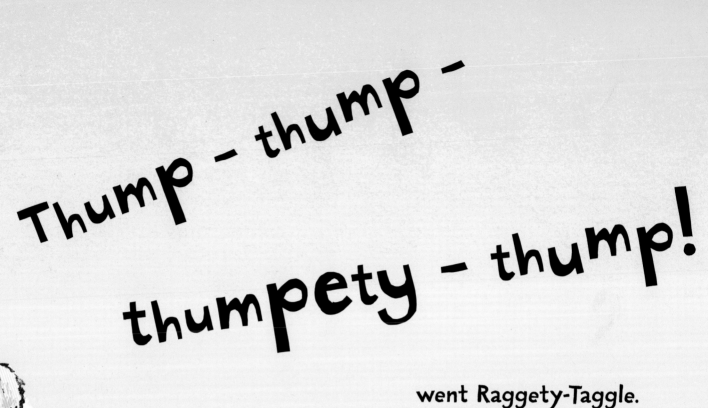

He didn't see that
the other rabbits had
swiftly, silently,
disappeared into their burrows.

The cat crouched.
The cat wriggled.

The cat . . .

MIAOW!
Hiss!

Raggety-Taggle
ran
for
his
life.

Through the cow field,

Mooo
oOOooO
OOOooo!

over the sheep pen,

Baa-baaaa!

Then as the cat
    chased after Raggety-Taggle . . .

. . . the dog chased after the cat . . .

WOOF!

. . . followed by the cows, **Moo!**

then the sheep, **Baa-baaaa!**

the horses, **Neigh!**

the pigs, **Oink! Oink!**

with the cockerel flapping behind . . .

Cock-a-doodle-do!

The angry farmer blew the tractor horn,

TOOT!

and everybody . . .

stopped.

All, that is, except for Raggety-Taggle,

who quietly tucked up his tail . . .

and ran . . .

and ran . . .

and ran . . .

all the way home.

Later that evening, as the sun went down
and the farmyard grew quiet,
slowly and silently . . .
the meadow filled with rabbits.

Raggety-Taggle nibbled peacefully
and wondered just why **anybody**
would **ever** want to make
a noise **at all**.

If you enjoyed reading this book, you will love:

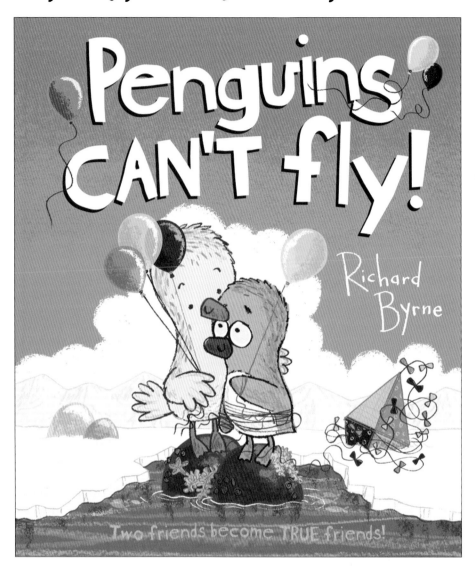

Penguins CAN'T fly!

Richard Byrne

Two friends become TRUE friends!

ISBN 9781849395137 (hardback)   9781849395687 (paperback)